This book belongs to

....

Copyright © 2020

make believe ideas ltd

The Wilderness, Berkhamsted, Hertfordshire, HP4 2AZ, UK.
501 Nelson Place, P.O. Box 141000, Nashville, TN 37214-1000, USA.

www.makebelieveideas.com

MY FIRST
playtime
TREASURY

make
believe
ideas

Contents

Never Touch a T. rex — 7

If You Ever See a Disco Fish — 31

Never Touch a Monster — 43

Funderpants! — 55

Unicorn's Magical Wishes — 83

Be Fabulous Like a Flamingo — 99

No Probllama — 111

Never Touch a Dinosaur 139

Oh No, Narwhal! 151

A Dazzle of Zebras 163

Never Touch a Dragon 187

Little Dino's Noisy Day 199

Never Touch a Shark 215

H is for Happy-saurus 227

NEVER touch A T. rex

Rosie Greening · Stuart Lynch

SECURITY

T. rex Team raptor

Hey, you!

I know why you're here.

You want to **touch** the **T. rex**, don't you?

WELL YOU CAN'T.

Here's the rule:

① You must never touch a T. rex, unless you . . .

. . . point to your nose.

There's no way you can point to your nose. Just you try!

How did you do that?

Okay, this is the real rule.
You must **never** touch a  **T. rex,**
unless you . . .

. . . POINT to your nose

and TOUCH your toes!

Ha! Try those if you
think you're so clever.

13

Okay, **genius.**

The **actual** rule is this:

Never touch a T. rex,

unless you . . .

SECURITY

T. rex
Team
Raptor

point to your nose,

touch your toes,

and find a rose. **?**

GOTCHA!

You won't find a rose on this page.

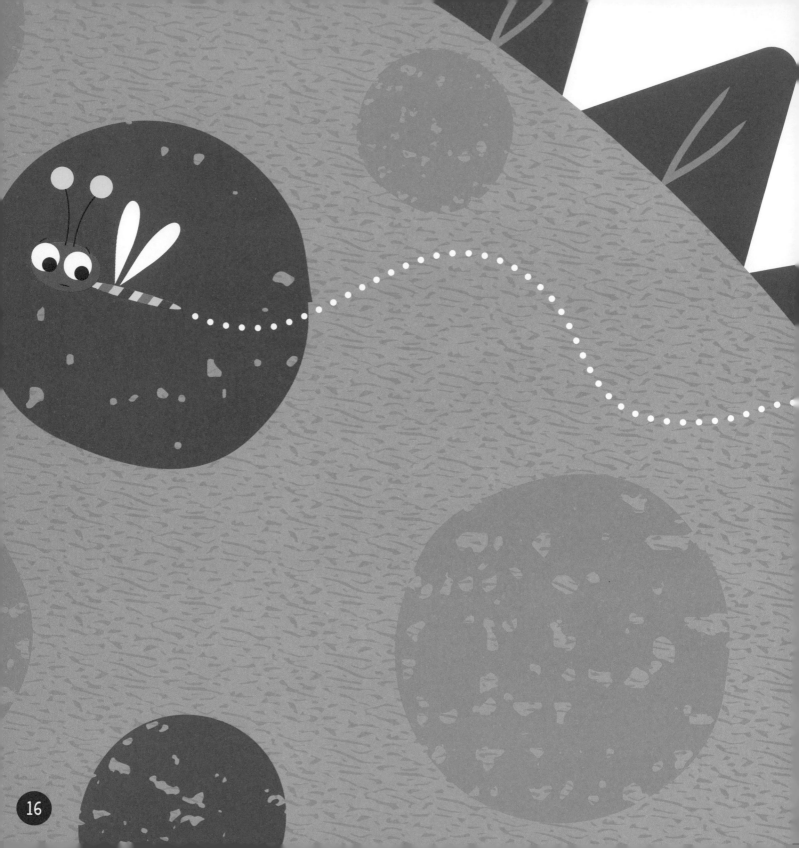

How are you DOING this?

Right. **EVEN YOU** won't be able to . . .

. . . point to your nose,

touch your toes,

find a rose,

and shout, "Banana!"

Have you done this before?

It's **lucky** I have a plan . . .

You must never touch a **T. rex,**
unless you . . . .

find a rose,

I COUNT 2
to three, 3

touch
your toes,

Wave
at me,

. . . point
to your
nose,

SHout,
"BANANA!"

GLUE

meow
like a cat,
SECURITY
FLAP
like a
BAT,
T.rex Team
Raptor
sing HIGH,
then low,
SAAAAAAAY
SOOOMETHIIIIING
SLOOOOOWWWW...

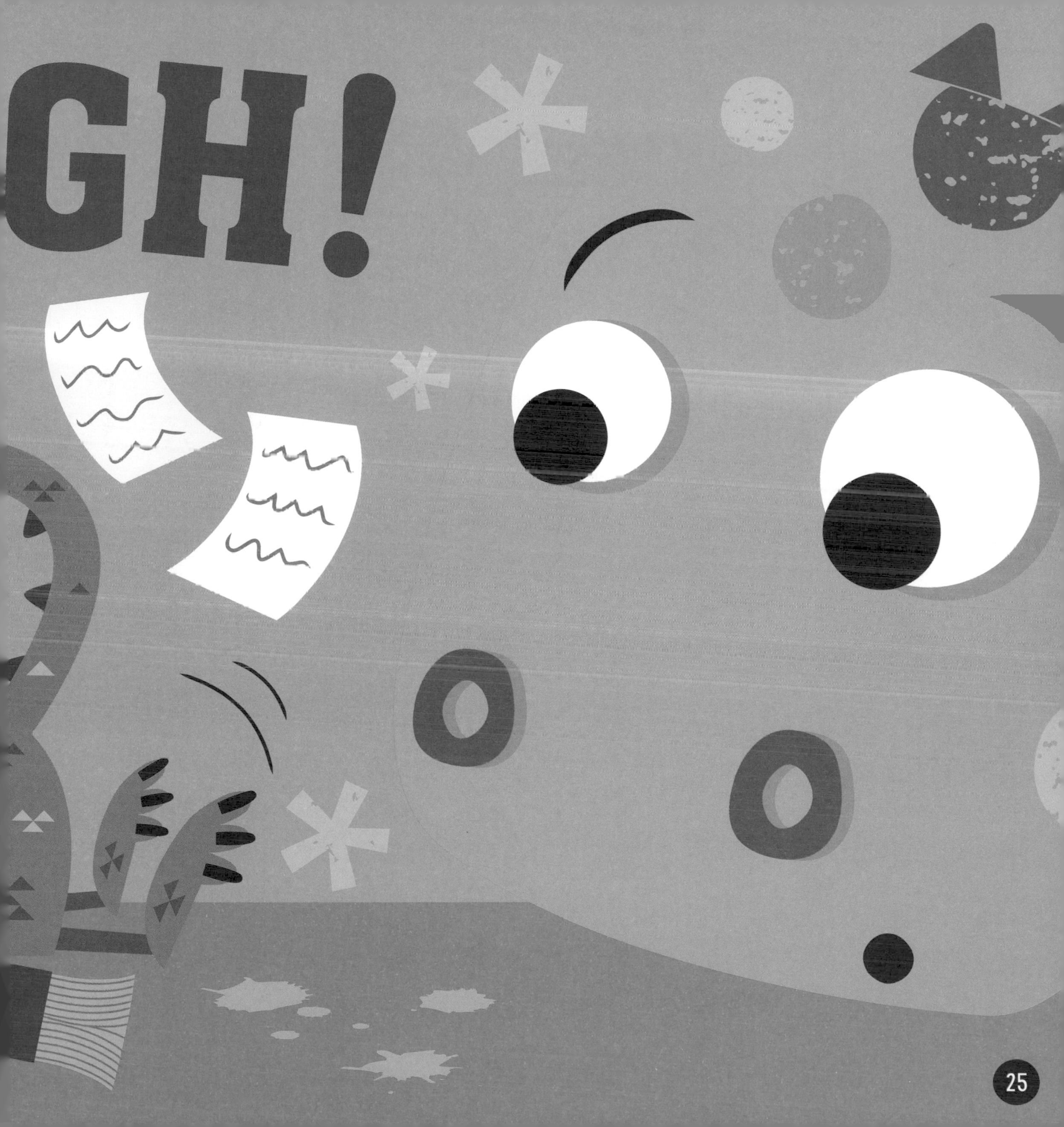
GH!

"HELLO!

Sorry about the guard.

There's really only one you need to know.

You must **never** touch a T. rex,
unless you . . .

ASK POLITELY.

Go on, **give it a try!**"

"How nice and polite you are!

OF COURSE YOU CAN!"

Okay, okay.

You're brighter than I thought.
But I've got one more rule for you:

DON'T CLOSE
this book!

THE END

If you ever see a Disco fish

Rosie Greening · Stuart Lynch

If you **ever** see a

Disco fish,

then **don't** give her a **wink**.

You'll make her feel **embarrassed**,

and her **scales** will

all turn **pink!**

If you **ever** see a

Disco fish,

please **don't** give him a **treat**.

He turns a sickly **green** each time

he tries to **dance** and **eat!**

Snack Bar

If you **ever** see a

Disco fish,

then **don't** play **hide**-and-**seek**.

She'll make her scales turn ocean **blue**

and **won't** be seen for weeks!

If you **ever** see a

Disco fish,

then **try** not to be **rude**.

He'll turn an **angry** shade of **red**

and swim off in a **mood!**

But if you **ever** see a

Disco fish,

there's **one** thing you **should** do.

Put on all of your

favorite songs,

and he will **dance** with you!

The end

NEVER touch A monster!

Rosie Greening · Stuart Lynch

You MUST NEVER TOUCH A **monster** who has SMILED at YOU and WAVED. It may look WARM and FRIENDLY, but it isn't WELL BEHAVED!

You MUST NEVER TOUCH A **monster** who has ASKED you ROUND for TEA. IT WANTS to put you IN A POT AND EAT YOU (probably).

You MUST NEVER TOUCH A **monster** - it's a SILLY thing TO DO! IGNORE it if it SMILES and SAYS, "Hello, there! HOW ARE YOU?"

You MUST NEVER TOUCH A **monster** – you should ALWAYS HURRY by. Just keep on WALKING PAST IT, and DON'T look it in THE EYE!

And DON'T EVER TOUCH A **monster** who is HUNGRY for its LUNCH. It MIGHT just SEE you COMING and decide to take a **munch!**

THE END

FUNDERPANTS!

James Dillon · Rosie Greening

Every llama looks the same.
No one knows each other's name.
Say hello to Llama Joe.

Actually, that's Moe.

This is how life goes for Joe:

Are you Moe?

NO, I'm JOE.

Are you FLO?

NO, I'm JOE.

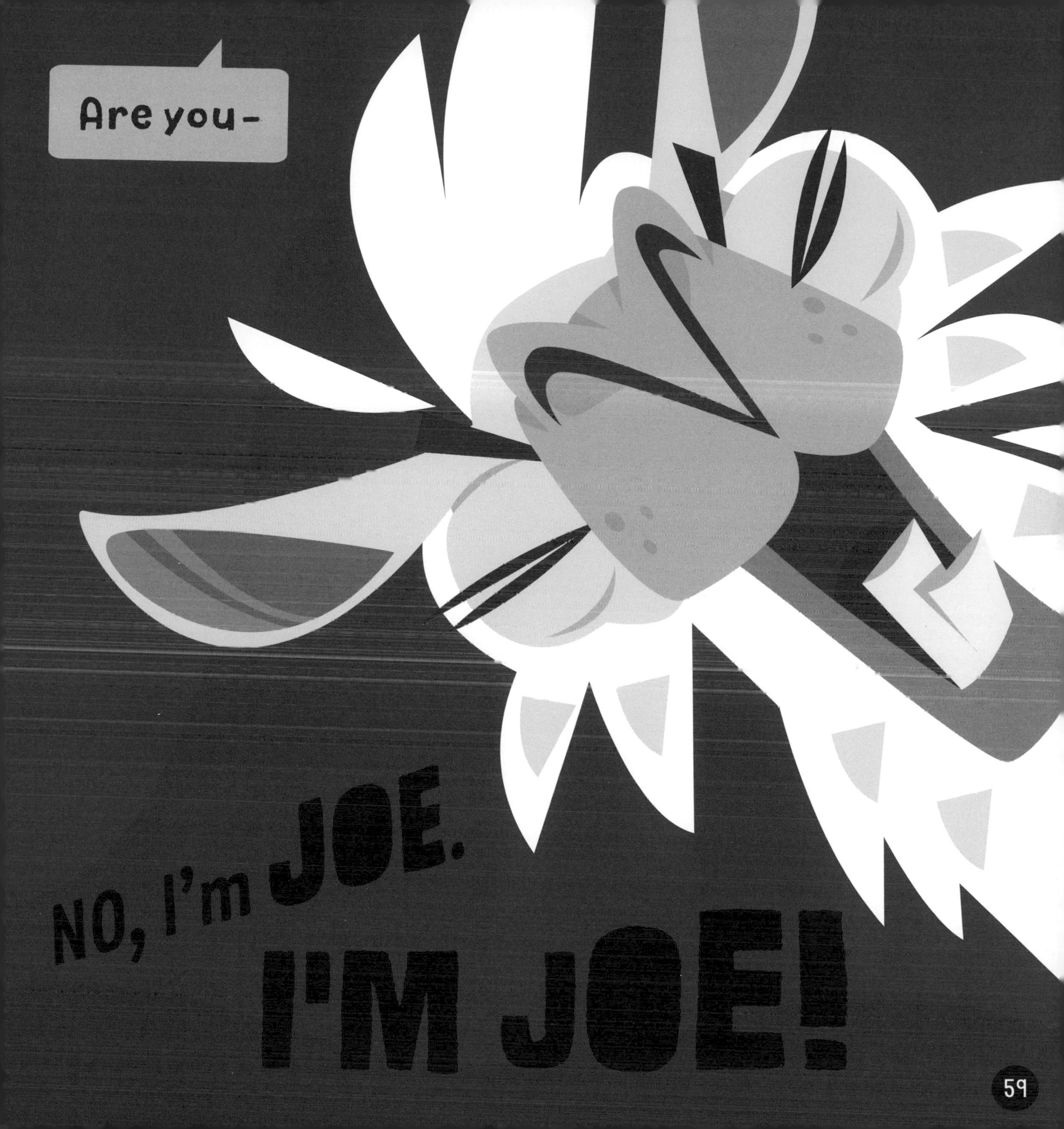
Are you-
NO, I'm JOE.
I'M JOE!

I've had enough.
This is **ABSURD**.

It's time to **STAND OUT**
from the **HERD!**

These **SUPER-STILTS** will make me **TALL.**

Slow down Joe, you're going to . . .

FALL!

63

If this plan **fails**,
I'll **EAT** my **hat**.

I'm **DONE!**

That's that.
I hate this hat.

I give up . . .

wait, **what is that?**

IDEA THREE

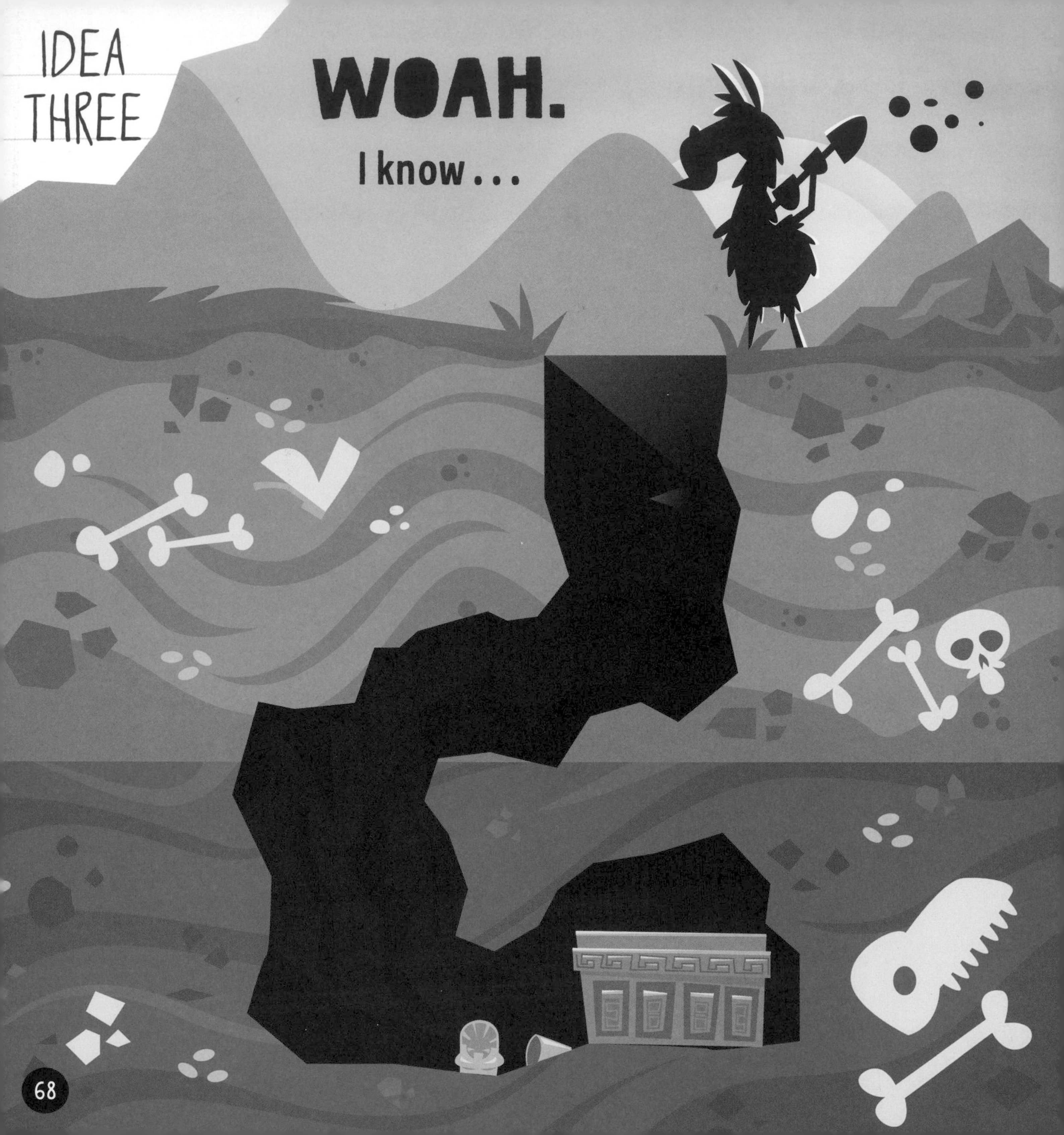

I'll wear this and GLOW against the FLOW!

69

The **HERD** are in for such a shock.

LOOK OUT, WORLD, JOE
it's JOE o'clock!

Now this is how life goes for Joe:
Get a load of Joe!
It's Joe!
I totally want a pair of those.
Woah, Joe!

But soon, Joe gets
a nasty blow.

He wakes up, yawns,

then . . .

75

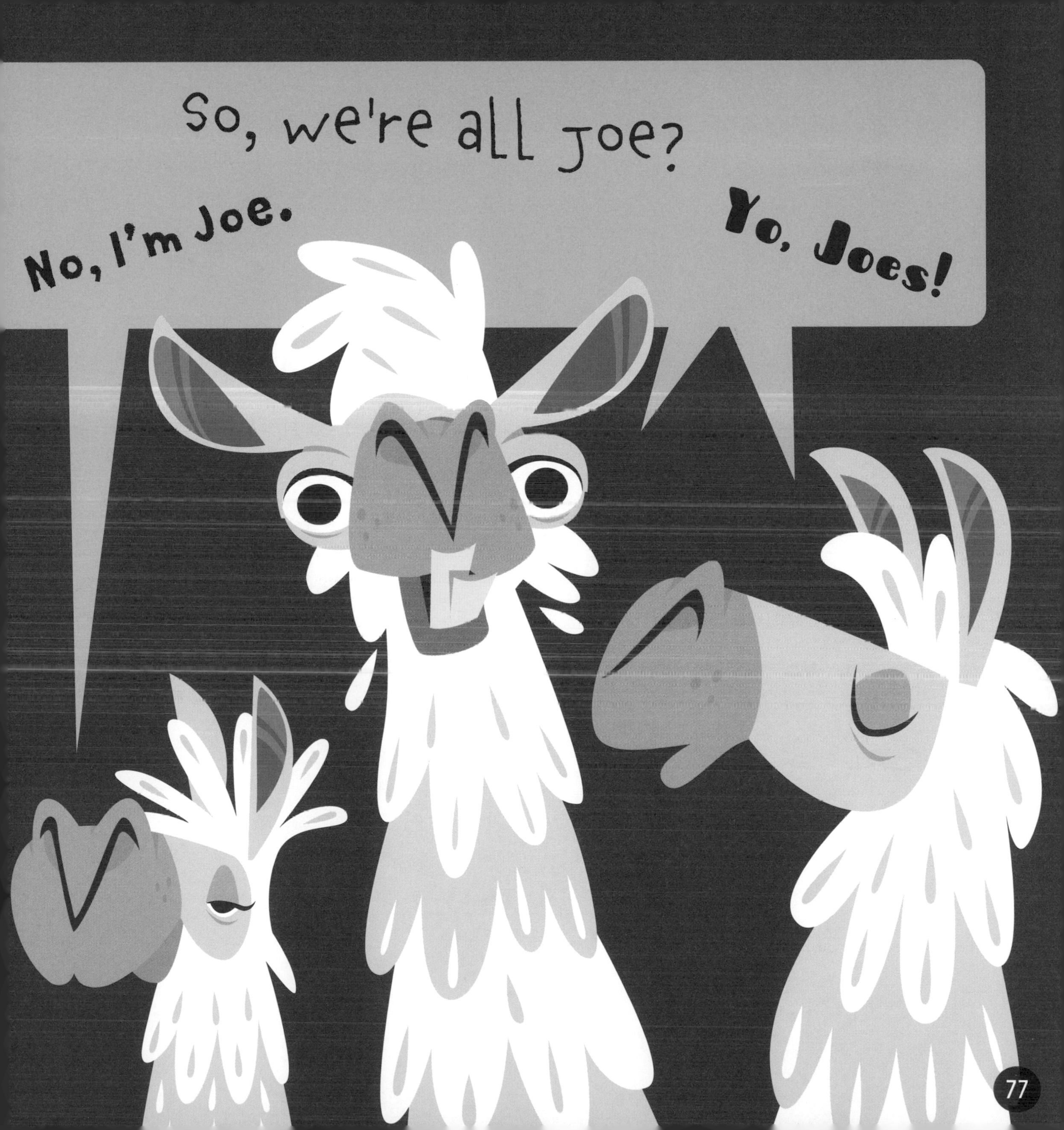
So, we're all Joe?
No, I'm Joe.
Yo, Joes!

But . . .

the REAL Joe knows
just what to do.

FUNDERPANTS

JOE

for **you** . . .

and **you!**

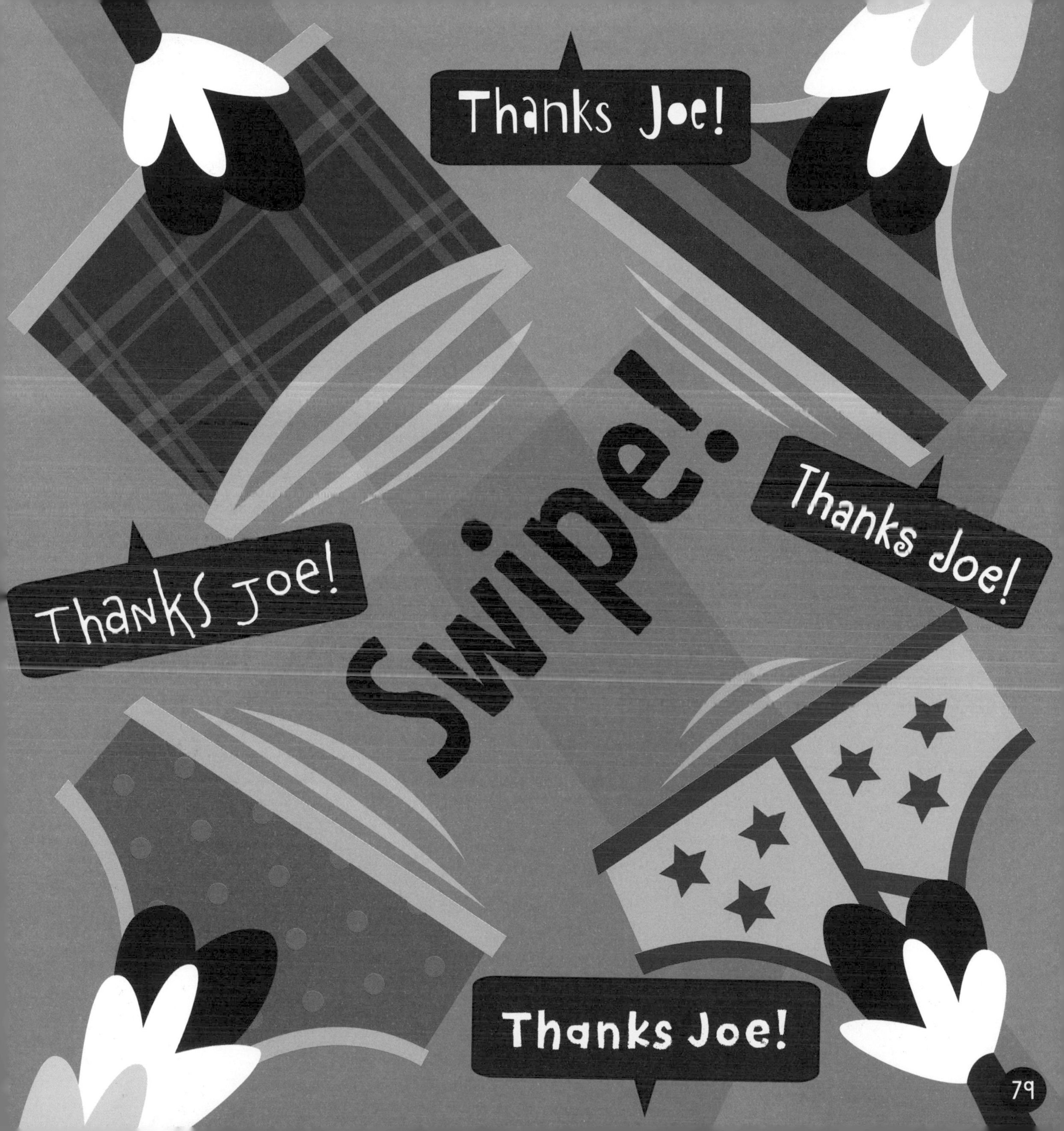
Thanks Joe!
Thanks Joe!
Swipe!
Thanks Joe!
Thanks Joe!

Now thanks to Joe, the herd all know . . .

The
END

Unicorn's
Magical Wishes

Rosie Greening · Dawn Machell

Sparkle was a very kind and magic **unicorn**.

Each day, she granted **wishes** with her twirly, swirly horn.

Little Fairy said,
"I wish for something **small** to eat."

So Sparkle waved her horn
to make a **tiny** strawberry treat.

Big, tall Giant said,
"I wish I had a **massive** snack."

So Sparkle swished her horn
to make the **largest** sandwich stack.

Fiery Dragon said,
"I wish for treats to **warm** me up."

So Sparkle twirled her horn
to make **hot chocolate** in a cup.

Snowy Yeti said,
"I wish for something very cold."

So Sparkle whirled her horn to make
a chilled ice cream to hold.

Sparkle felt a little **sad** now she was all alone.

She swirled her horn once more
to grant a wish all of her own...

In a flash, her friends appeared,
with special cupcakes too.

"Now I'm **happy**," Sparkle said.
"My wishes have come true!"

The end

Be Fabulous LIKE A FLAMINGO!

James Dillon · Rosie Greening

I'M A FABULOUS

FLAMINGO.

THERE'S NOTHING I CAN'T DO.

IF YOU STICK OUT OF THE flock,

THEN YOU CAN BE FAB, TOO!

I'M A SUPER-SPLENDID SLOTH.

I LIVE life AT SL-O-O-O-W PACE.

TAKE TIME TO smell

THE roses: IT'S A JOURNEY,

NOT A race!

I'M A CHAMPION CHAMELEON.

I'M SUCH A JAZZY SIGHT.

SO, SHOW OFF YOUR TRUE COLORS,

AND YOU'LL FIND THAT

LIFE IS bright!

I'M AN OUTSTANDING

orangutan.

I HAVE fun EVERY DAY.

IF YOU LIKE TO GO BANANAS,

YOU CAN live YOUR

LIFE THIS WAY!

I'M A PERFECT

peacock.

I WAS BORN TO BE A star.

NO MATTER WHAT, REMEMBER

TO BE PROUD OF WHO YOU are!

THE END

No Probllama!

Rosie Greening · Kali Stileman

Llama loved to **boast**. "I'm **faster** than **you**," he told Cheetah.

LL4M4

112

Every day, Lemur watched on and tried to **ignore** Llama.

But he **really** . . .

hated . . .

...show-offs!

One morning, Lemur decided to put Llama to the **test**.

"Oi, Llama!" he shouted. "Can you **paint?**"

"Can you do **Karate?**"

119

"Can you talk underwater?"

"Can you sing . . .

whilst standing
on your head?"

123

"Can you swing like a **monkey?**"

"No prob-

llee-ee-

oo-oo-

aama!"

"Can you drink **tea** on a **surfboard?**"

"Can you do
ballet...

on a
mountain...

...in a **snowstorm?**"

"No probrrr brrrrrr-llama!"

"Can you **skydive**?"

"No problllaaaamaaaa!"

133

"Do you know how to get **home?**"

"No prob lemur!"

NEVER touch A dinosaur!

Rosie Greening · Stuart Lynch

You MUST NEVER TOUCH A dinosaur with SPINES along its BACK. Just say "GOOD-BYE!" and WALK ON BY – it might think you're a SNACK!

You MUST NEVER TOUCH A dinosaur with HORNS upon its HEAD. It's not a CAT, so DO NOT PAT – just LOOK AWAY instead!

You MUST NEVER TOUCH A dinosaur with SHARP and POINTY CLAWS. Just GO and HIDE somewhere INSIDE, and please LOCK all the doors!

You MUST NEVER TOUCH A dinosaur with GIANT, bony PLATES. A friendly PAT is SOMETHING that this DINO really HATES!

But IF YOU EVER TOUCH A dinosaur (which REALLY won't be FUN), please ASK it next, "Are you T. REX?" and if it nods, then RUN!

149

THE END

Oh NO, Narwhal!

Lara Ede · Rosie Greening

It's a tough life being Narwhal.

His tusk gets in the way!

Look out!

"Oh NO, Narwhal!"
cry his friends,

School

each time he tries to play.

153

If **Narwhal** plays with **Dolphin**,
he makes the ball go . . .

POP!

When it's time for **hide**-and-**seek**,
his **tusk** gives him away.

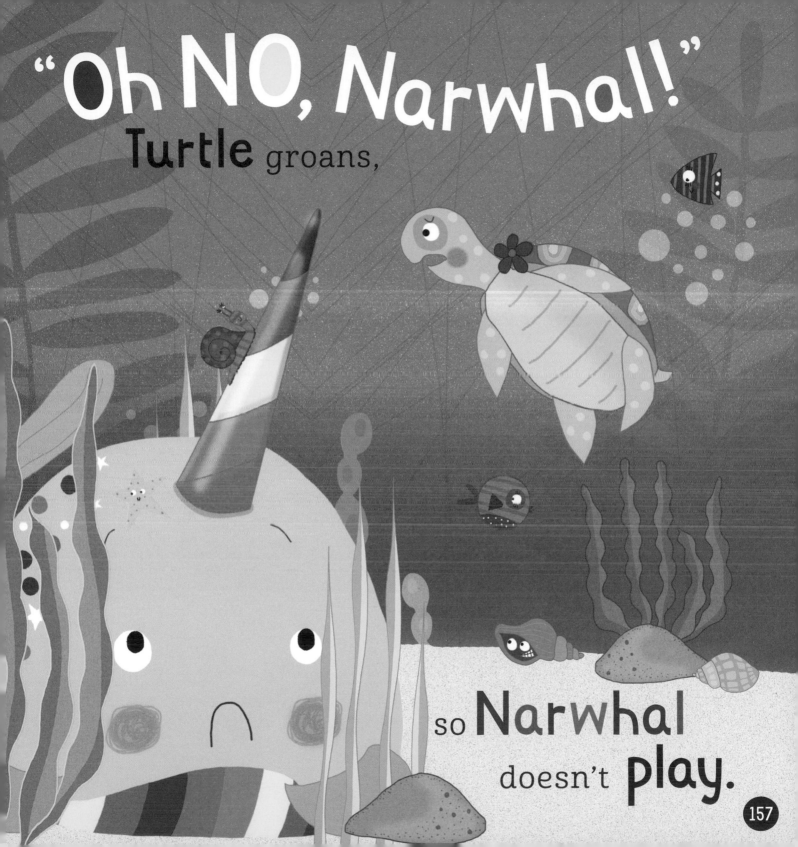

"Oh NO, Narwhal!"
Turtle groans,

so **Narwhal**
doesn't **play.**

When they are playing **music**, Narwhal gets into a **spin.**

"Oh NO, Narwhal!" Crab cries out,

so **Narwhal** can't join in.

159

At last, the group finds something
Narwhal knows that he can do.

DOLPHIN 60 TURTLE 60

160

"Oh YES, Narwhal!"

cry his friends.

"This is the game for you!"

The end

A DAZZLE of ZEBRAS

Sarah Creese · Stephanie Thannhauser

A family of animals is called a special word:

a **FLOCK** of **SHEEP**,

A FLOCK OF SHEEP

a **PACK** of **WOLVES**,

A PACK OF WOLVES

or **COWS**, a mooing **HERD**.

Have you heard of cows?

A HERD OF COWS

Each group has
a different name;
there are many
more to see.
Let's turn the page
to meet them all –
it's showtime now
for…

ME!

ZEBRAS are a DAZZLE
in their showbiz black and whites.

A DAZZLE OF ZEBRAS

PORCUPINES are
a **PRICKLE**—
but they're
perfectly polite.

ELEPHANTS
blow their trumpets
in a trunk-to-tail
PARADE.

A BASK OF CROCODILES

CROCODILES are a BASK,

hanging out in shorts and shades.

171

GORILLAS are a noisy **BAND**

A CRASH OF RHINOS

and **RHINOS**
make a
CRASH!

BATS fly in a CAULDRON,

A CAULDRON OF BATS

174

making potions fizz and flash.

PENGUINS are a PARCEL, neatly tied up with a bow.

3 + 3 = 6

A SCHOOL OF FISH

FISH become a swimming SCHOOL, learning on the go!

I'm going to be a STARfish!

A TOWER OF GIRAFFES

GIRAFFES stand in a **TOWER,** teetering up from hoof to head.

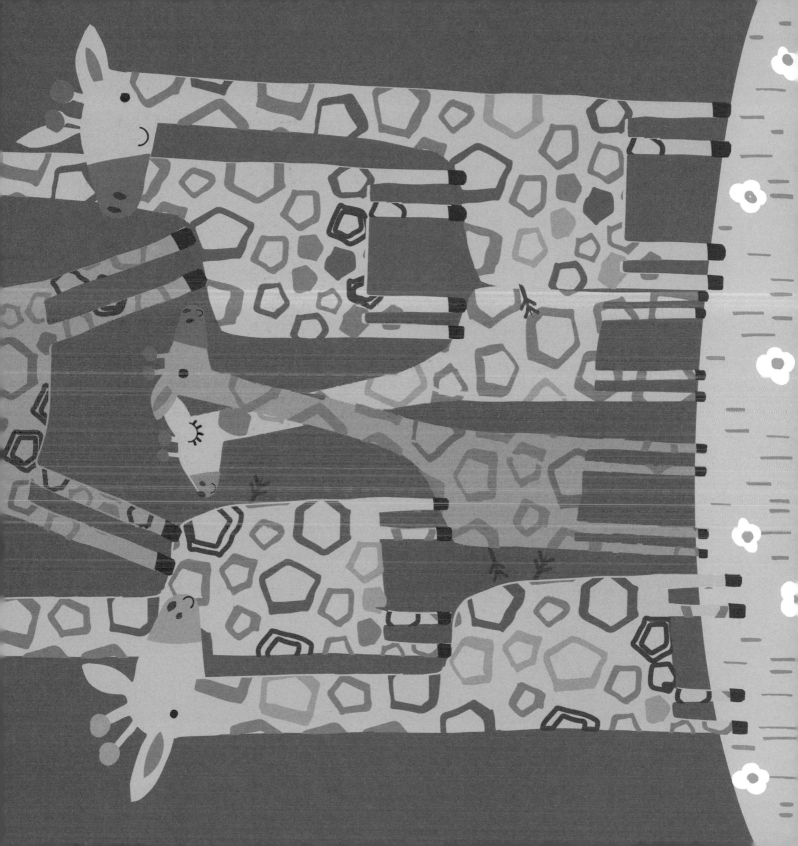

TOADS prefer to tie up in a slimy **KNOT** instead.

A KNOT OF TOADS

180

 BUZZ TIMETABLE
Route 1 07:33 12:42 16:27
Route 7 09:15 11:39 13:58

 A BUSINESS OF FLIES

FLIES become a BUSINESS, doing jobs for all the bugs.

HIGH-FLYERS OF THE MONTH

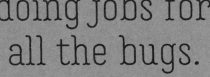

 FLYING TIPS

SHARKS swim in a **SHIVER**,

I'm sooo cool.

Stop brrrragging

so they need some extra hugs!

The world is full
of **ANIMALS**.
How many can you see?

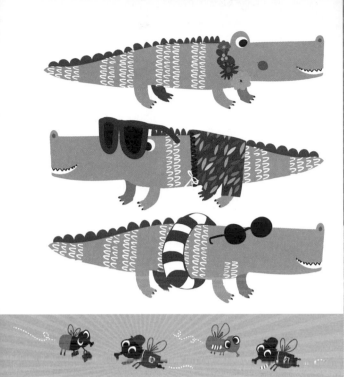

Now choose the **GROUP** you like the best.

Which **ONE** will it be?

185

NEVER *touch* A dragon!

Rosie Greening · Stuart Lynch

You MUST NEVER TOUCH A **dragon** that has **CURVY,** curly **CLAWS.** **DISTRACT** it with a **SANDWICH,** and then **RUN AWAY** indoors!

You MUST NEVER TOUCH A dragon with a TWISTY, twirly TAIL. Just hang a SIGN around its NECK and put it up FOR SALE!

You MUST NEVER TOUCH A dragon that has WEIRD and wavy WINGS. Just LEAVE it with a MICROPHONE and SNEAK OFF while it SINGS!

You MUST NEVER TOUCH A dragon that has LUMPY, bumpy SKIN. Just turn your HOUSE into a FORT that DRAGONS can't GET IN!

And DON'T EVER TOUCH A dragon with a SMOKY, sparking SNOUT.

Just find a HOSE and splash its NOSE before the flames come out!

THE END

Little Dino's Noisy Day

Rosie Greening · Stuart Lynch

One day, Danny heard a BOOM
he'd never heard before.

BOOM!

"What was that?" he wondered, and he set off to explore.

Danny soon found Tilly,
who was **stomping** round with glee.

"Did you go BOOM?" asked Danny.
But she said, "It wasn't me!"

STOMP!

Danny kept on walking
and saw Victor **whoosh** ahead.

WHOOOO

"Did you go BOOM?" asked Danny.
But Victor shook his head.

Nearby, Dawn was **crunching** leaves,
and standing big and tall.

"Did you go BOOM?" asked Danny.
But Dawn said, "Not at all!"

CRUNCH!

Danny soon saw T. rex Tom,
the grumpy dinosaur.

"Did you go BOOM?" asked Danny.
But Tom just gave a ROARRR!

ROARRR!

Danny Dino then looked up
at something big and red.

The volcano gave a noisy BOOM.
"That's it!" Danny said.

211

He turned to go, then heard a CRACK.
"What was that?" he said.

RACK!

So Danny Dino headed off
to find that sound instead!

The end

NEVER *touch* A shark!

Rosie Greening · Stuart Lynch

You MUST NEVER TOUCH A GIANT shark who's in a SNAPPY mood. But if he bakes FIN-TASTIC TREATS, then you can try his FOOD!

You MUST NEVER TOUCH AN octopus- it might RUIN your day. But if she has a PACK of CARDS, it's fine for you to PLAY.

You MUST NEVER TOUCH A **seahorse** - it's <u>NOT</u> a good IDEA. But if she's in a swimming RACE, then you CAN

WAVE and CHEER!

You MUST NEVER TOUCH A **puffer fish** in CASE he's going to BLOW. But if it is his BIRTHDAY, you should STOP and SAY, "HELLO!"

So, NEVER TOUCH A sea creature who ISN'T in this RHYME. But if it's in a BUOY BAND, you can join in EVERY TIME!

THE END

H IS FOR HAPPY-SAURUS

James Dillon · Holly Lansley

B

BRAVE-asaur

tries things, even
when she's scared.

C

CALM-otaurus
keeps his cool.

-odon

hopes no one noticed.

Eek!

232

F... fears the worst.

-OCUS

GUILTY-ophus
knows he's in the wrong.

DO NOT EAT!

H

HAPPY-saurus
is one delighted dino!

235

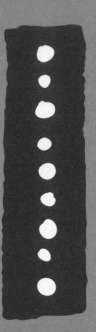

IMPATIENT-tops

hates to wait.

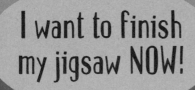

I want to finish my jigsaw NOW!

JEALOUS-saurus
wants what others have.

237

K

KIND-odon
is considerate and caring.

LAZY-saur
loves to lie down.

239

M

MOODY-mimus
gets in a grump.

Isn't this alphabet over yet?